Great•Aunt•Martha

by rebecca c. jones
illustrated by shelley jackson

dutton children's books   new york

For Loretta Beth Castaldi,
now tottering through her fifth decade
r . j .

_____

For Caroline, who helped me finish,
and my grandmothers, who helped me start
s . j .

Text copyright © 1995 by Rebecca C. Jones
Illustrations © 1995 by Shelley Jackson

Library of Congress Cataloging-in-Publication Data

Jones, Rebecca C.
Great-Aunt Martha / by Rebecca C. Jones;
illustrated by Shelley Jackson. — 1st ed.
p. cm.
Summary: A young girl cannot watch television, dance,
or play with the dog because her parents think that a visiting
great-aunt needs her rest.
ISBN 0-525-45257-5
[1. Great-aunts — Fiction. 2. Old age — Fiction.]
I. Jackson, Shelley, ill. II. Title.
PZ7.J72478Gr 1994
[E] — dc20 93-43958 CIP AC

Published in the United States in 1995 by Dutton Children's Books,
a division of Penguin Books USA Inc.,
375 Hudson Street, New York, New York 10014
Designed by Sara Reynolds
Printed in Mexico
First Edition
1 3 5 7 9 10 8 6 4 2

Great-Aunt Martha
was coming.

So Mama washed the windows,
Papa vacuumed the floors,
and I had to pick up every single toy.

We went to the store and bought fish
and carrots and spinach and prune juice.
"No pizza or pretzels today," Mama said,
"because Great-Aunt Martha is coming."

———— ❀ ————

Papa shaved in the middle of the day,

Mama curled her hair,

and I had to take a bath,
because Great-Aunt Martha was coming.

Then Great-Aunt Martha came.

She didn't look so great.
She just looked old.

She hugged Papa.
She hugged Mama.
She even hugged me.
"Is this the baby?" she asked.
"My, how she's grown!"

Papa took her suitcases.
Mama gave her a glass of lemonade.
They all sat in the living room
and talked about weather and airplanes
and people I never knew.

Great-Aunt Martha yawned (and so did I).
"You must be very tired," Papa told her.
"Yes," Mama said. "You need your rest."
Great-Aunt Martha sighed and
went to her room.

I turned on the TV to watch cartoons.

But Mama said to turn it off
because Great-Aunt Martha was here
and she needed her rest.

❁

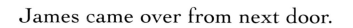

James came over from next door.

But Mama said we couldn't play
because Great-Aunt Martha was here
and she needed her rest.

I turned on some music so I could dance.

But Papa said to turn it off
because Great-Aunt Martha was here
and she needed her rest.

I rolled a ball for Skipper to chase.

Skipper barked (just once)
and Papa put him in the garage
because Great-Aunt Martha was here
and she needed her rest.

Finally, Great-Aunt Martha came out
of her room, and we ate dinner.
We had fish and carrots and spinach
and prune juice.
Great-Aunt Martha said it was delicious.

But it wasn't.

Then everyone sat down in the living room
and talked about weather and airplanes
and people I never knew.

Great-Aunt Martha yawned (and so did I).

"It's been a long day," Papa said.

"Yes," Mama said. "We all need our rest."

Great-Aunt Martha stayed in her room
a long time in the morning.
I knew I couldn't turn on the TV.
I knew I couldn't invite James over.
I knew I couldn't dance to my music.
I knew I couldn't play with Skipper.
I knew I had to be very, very quiet
because Great-Aunt Martha was here
and she needed her rest.

Then we heard a tap-tap-tap
coming from Great-Aunt Martha's room.
It got louder and L O U D E R and L O U D E R.

We tiptoed to the door of Great-Aunt Martha's room, and we opened it.

"Be careful!" Mama cried.

"You'd better sit down," Papa warned,
"before you fall down!"

There was Great-Aunt Martha—
dancing with her cane.
"This place is too quiet!" she shouted.
"I don't want to sit and
I don't want to talk and
I definitely do not want to rest!
Let's make some noise
and have some fun!"

So Papa turned on the music,
and Mama turned on the TV,
and I invited James over,

and Skipper came in from the garage,
and Great-Aunt Martha ordered pizza.
We all had a party...

because Great-Aunt Martha was here —
and she really was great!